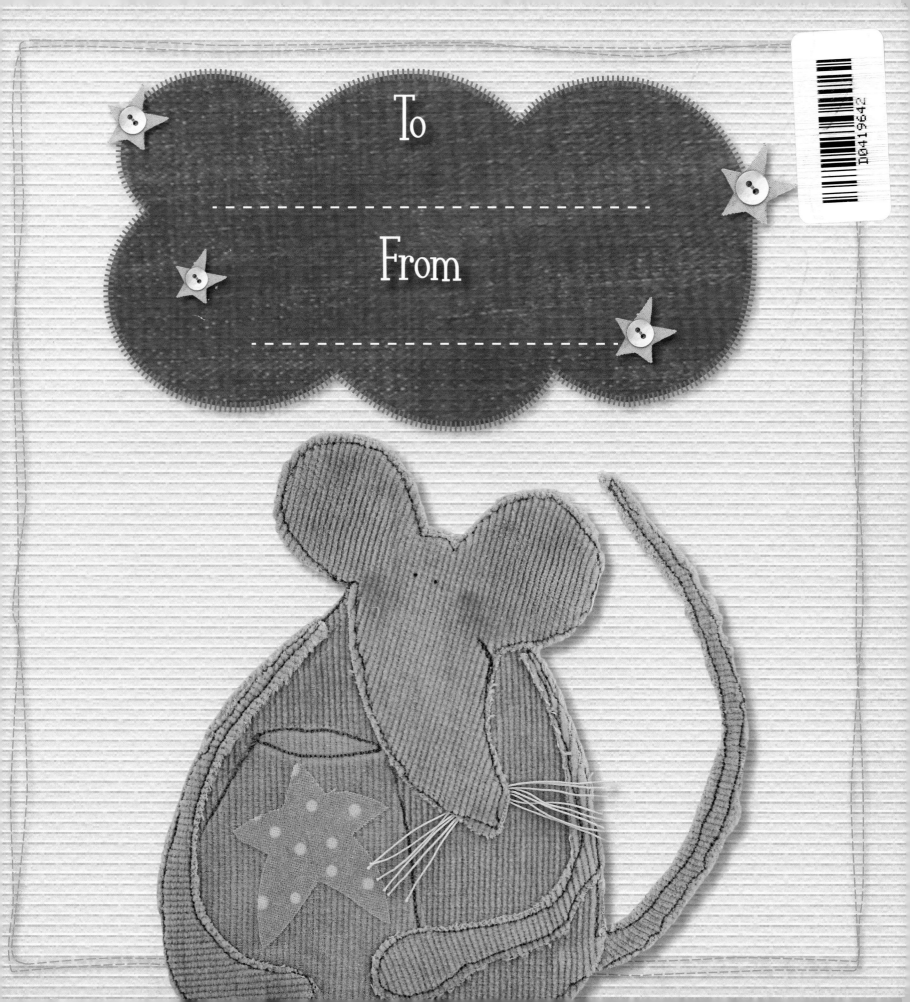

To

From

Twinkle Twinkle Little Star

Kate Toms

make
believe
ideas

Twinkle, twinkle,

little **star**,

how I wonder

what **you** are,

you **shine** above the **world** so high, like a **lightbulb** in the **sky**.

I'd love to catch you in my net . . .

and keep you as a special pet!

Twinkle, twinkle, little **star**, I do so **wonder** what **you** are.

When snuggled up in **bed** at night,

cozy, **warm**, and **tucked** up tight,

I dream that I can fly
a rocket . . .

5 4 3 2

and gather
stardust in my pocket.

Twinkle, twinkle, little **star**, how I wonder what **you** are.

Does a **man** live on the **moon?**

And if the moon is made of cheese,

Yummy!

will you save some for me, please?

Twinkle, twinkle, little star,
what do you see from afar?

¡Hola!

Hello!

Are there **stars** for us **all** up there?

All mine!

Wheeeeee!

Jump!

Or do some folks have to share?

Twinkle, twinkle, little **star**, how I wonder what **you** are!

When the **sky** grows **dark** at night, I **wish** and **wish** with all my **might**,

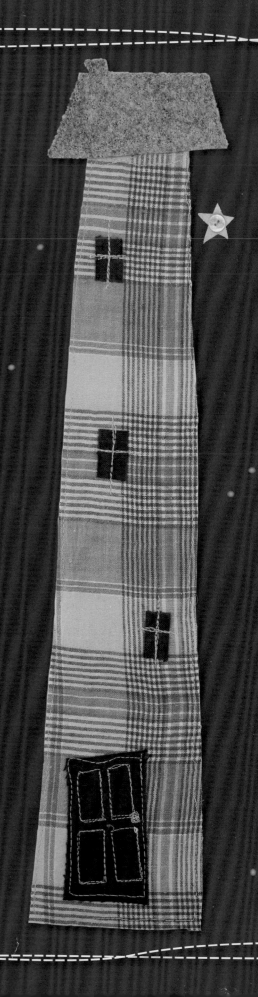

that you would look down
on my **house**,
and grant one thing
for this small **mouse**.

I want to be a **star** like you,

Wheeeeeeeeee!

and see the **world** the way you do.

Twinkle, twinkle, little star,
how I wonder what you are.

When it's time to climb the stairs,

to brush my teeth
and say my prayers,

through my window, I can see
that you are smiling down on me.

Twinkle, twinkle, little **star**, how I wonder what **you** are,